LETTERS HOME
from
SCOTLAND

Marcia S. Gresko

BLACKBIRCH PRESS, INC.
WOODBRIDGE, CONNECTICUT

Published by Blackbirch Press, Inc.
260 Amity Road
Woodbridge, CT 06525

©2000 by Blackbirch Press, Inc.
First Edition

e-mail: staff@blackbirch.com
Web site: www.blackbirch.com

Printed in Singapore

10 9 8 7 6 5 4 3 2 1

Photo Credits: Cover and title page inset: ©Bruce Glassman. Pages 4, 8, 9, 12, 13, 14 (left), 15, 29, 31: ©Bruce Glassman. All other photographs ©Corel Corporation.

Library of Congress Cataloging-in-Publication Data

Gresko, Marcia S.
   Scotland / by Marcia S. Gresko.
   p. cm. — (Letters home from . . .)
   Includes bibliographical references and index.
   Summary: Describes some of the sights and experiences on a trip to Scotland, including visits to Edinburgh, Loch Ness, Ben Nevis, Skye, and Glasgow.
   ISBN 1-56711-408-3
   1. Scotland—Juvenile literature. [1. Scotland—Description and travel.] I. Title.
DA762 .G74 2000   99-041814
941.1—dc21   CIP

TABLE OF CONTENTS

Arrival in . . .

Edinburgh

After a long flight and a stopover in London, England, we finally arrived in Edinburgh—Scotland's capital city. Scotland, like England, Wales, and Northern Ireland, is part of the United Kingdom of Great Britain and Northern Ireland. People usually just say Great Britain, United Kingdom, or U.K.

According to our guidebook, Scotland is a small country, about the size of South Carolina. More than 700 islands lie off its long, jagged coastline. There are also lively cities, busy ports, and ancient—some say haunted—castles.

Exploring Scotland during the summer is great. Because it's located so far north, there are as many as 18 to 20 hours of sunlight each day. We'll have lots of time to see the sights!

Edinburgh

Visiting Edinburgh is like traveling to two cities at once! The city is divided into two parts—Old Town and New Town.

Our hotel is in New Town. Princes Street, Edinburgh's main thoroughfare, is close by. On one side of it are fashionable shops and department stores. On the other are flower-filled gardens. New Town also has broad streets and elegant public squares. It's got grand old homes, and major museums and monuments. Two monuments honor Scotland's great writers—Sir Walter Scott and the beloved national poet, Robert Burns. Literature is Scotland's richest art form.

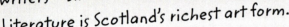

Canongate Tolisooth Royal Mile

Princes Street Gardens

Princes Street

Edinburgh

Old Town is the historic heart of Edinburgh. Its main street is called the Royal Mile. It links the city's two great landmarks—the 900-year-old Edinburgh Castle and the Palace of Holyroodhouse. Nearby, narrow, winding streets lead to medieval churches, grand public buildings, and crowded tenement neighborhoods. According to the guidebook, "The Strange Case of Dr. Jekyll and Mr. Hyde," by Scottish author Robert Louis Stevenson, is based on a real criminal who lived near here.

Edinburgh has other neat sights. There's a statue to Greyfriar's Bobby, a dog who stayed by its master's grave for 14 years, leaving only for food. And the zoo has the largest number of penguins in captivity anywhere!

Edinburgh Castle

Built on an extinct volcano, Edinburgh Castle seems to guard the city. This 11th-century castle has been a home, a fort, and a prison.

There was lots to see there! Tiny St. Margaret's Chapel is the oldest surviving building in Edinburgh. Mary Queen of Scots gave birth in the Royal Apartments to a son who became a king of England. In the Crown Room are the Honours of Scotland—the dazzling royal crown, scepter, and sword. In the case with the Honours is the sacred Stone of Destiny, on which the kings of Scotland were crowned.

Guard at Edinburgh Castle

Castle high above Edinburgh

Castle coat of arms

King Bruce statue

The best part of our visit was in the evening when the Castle Esplanade became the scene for the Military Tattoo. Military bands in their colorful tartans, bagpipers, and drummers paraded and performed. The event is part of the world-famous Edinburgh Festival, which is a three-week-long summer "happening" with music, dance, plays, films, and fireworks.

St. Andrews

It was a 50-mile bus ride northeast from Edinburgh to the city of St. Andrews. St. Andrews is known as the home of Scotland's oldest university. It's also the place where the game of golf was invented!

Our first stop was the ancient St. Rule's Tower. This city was "accidentally" founded by St. Rule. He was commanded by an angel to build a city honoring St. Andrew, when he was shipwrecked nearby.

Next door to the Tower are the ruins of St. Andrew's Cathedral. It was once the country's largest cathedral and its religious capital. At the remains of nearby St. Andrew's Castle, our guide pointed out the grim "bottle dungeon." It's a 24-foot pit carved from solid rock where prisoners spent their final days.

St. Andrews (from St. Rule's tower)

Aberdeen

From St. Andrews, we traveled 80 miles northeast to Aberdeen. It's Scotland's third-largest city, and has been a busy fishing port for nearly 1,000 years. It is also the main farming and industrial center for northern Scotland.

Strolling around the city, we could see how Aberdeen earned its nickname—"the granite city." Most of its buildings are built from sparkling white or silver local granite. One building, Marischal College, is the second-largest granite building in the world!

Aberdeen, city of granite and roses

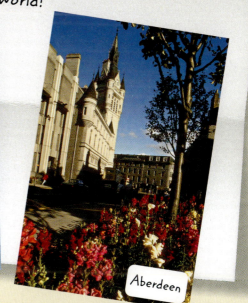

Aberdeen

Highlands

Highland scenery is awesome! The view from our tour bus window is always changing—mountains, valleys, moors, rivers, and lakes (called lochs).

The rugged scenery is beautiful, but it makes the Highlands a harsh place to live. The Highlands cover more than 66% of Scotland, but is its least populated area. Most Highlanders are hard-working sheep farmers. Collies and sheepdogs, both specially bred in Scotland, police their herds.

These hills are also home to castle ruins and crumbling watchtowers.

Highland sheep

Rough landscape

Highland scenery

Highland houses

These are reminders of the area's stormy history. Our guide explained that powerful groups, called clans, ruled the Highlands for more than 700 years. Members of a clan were considered sons of its chieftain, or leader. That's why so many Scottish last names begin with "Mac," which means "son of." Fierce, rival clans often feuded with one another over land or cattle.

Yesterday, we attended a traditional festival called the Highland Games. Originally these were contests where clan chieftains chose their best soldiers from among the winners. Today, skilled athletes still compete in events like tossing the caber (throwing a heavy log), putting the shot (heaving a heavy stone), and throwing the hammer.

River Spey

We've been exploring Strathspey, the valley of the River Spey. The Spey is Scotland's second-longest river. It rises in the Highlands and flows for about 100 miles northeast into the North Sea.

Strathspey's beautiful countryside is a favorite for sports fans. In the winter, there is great skiing. In the summer, there are all kinds of watersports. We've been enjoying the hiking and salmon fishing. With its many lakes and rivers, and more than 2,000 miles of coastline, fishing is an important Scottish industry. People in Scotland eat lots of fish. They even eat kippers (smoked herring) for breakfast!

Spey garden

River Spey

Whisky Industry

Scotland has a drink named after it! It's called Scotch, or Scotch whisky. The Scots have been making whisky for more than 500 years. There are so many whisky distilleries surrounding the River Spey that the region is known as the "whisky triangle."

Today we took a tour of one of the distilleries that makes Scotch whisky. According to our guide, the River Spey's clear rushing waters are the fastest-flowing in Great Britain. They are very important in the distilling process. So is locally grown barley, which is dried over peat fires. This is supposed to produce the finest whisky in the world. Scotland exports millions of gallons of Scotch each year—most of it to the United States.

Whisky stills

Inverness

We've been staying in the port city of Inverness, the commercial capital of the Highland Region.

The city is located on the River Ness. It's surrounded by hills on three sides. The city's strategic position has made it an important site since ancient times. We visited prehistoric stone burial chambers and the ruins of a fort. In medieval times, Inverness became a rich market center.

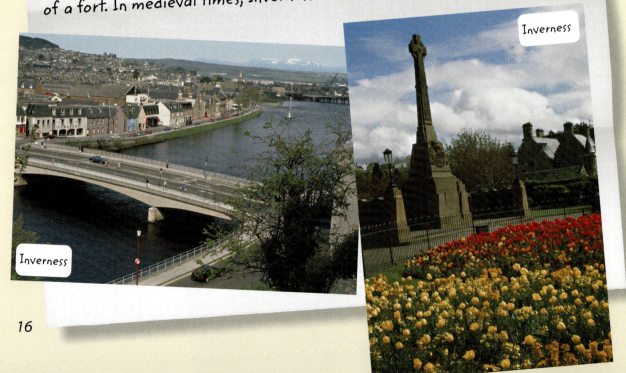

Inverness

Inverness

Inverness Castle

Inverness footbridge

Ships from Europe crowded its sheltered harbor, trading for leather, salmon, and timber. We visited 200-year-old Inverness Castle today. It stands on the site of several earlier castles. The world's greatest playwright, William Shakespeare, based his famous play "MacBeth," on events in this troubled place.

Loch Ness

The cruise boat to Loch Ness was super-crowded. Thousands of tourists visit the area each year hoping to snap a photo of "Nessie." That's what locals call the Loch Ness monster. It has also been given a scientific name—Nessitera rhombopteryx.

According to our guide, if Nessie is real, she is more than 1,400 years old! The first sighting of a "sea beast" in the lake was by a 6th-century saint. It is said that St. Columba (who introduced Christianity to Scotland) rescued one of his followers from the beast's attack by calming it with prayer.

Loch
Ness

Loch Ness monster sculpture

Since then, hundreds of people have reported seeing the "monster." Most agree that it is between 20 and 40 feet long, has flippers, 1 or 2 humps, and a long, slender neck and tail. Some think the creature may be a dinosaur-like reptile, maybe even a survivor from prehistoric times! Others suggest it is related to a modern-day sea animal such as a manatee or a giant sea snake.

Scientists have used many unsuccessful methods to solve the mystery, such as aerial photography, sonar surveys, and even small submarines. But Loch Ness is Scotland's largest lake. It makes an awfully good hiding place!

Ben Nevis

The area around Fort William was our next stop. It has been called "the land of glens, bens, and heroes." It's in the western end of Glen More called the Great Glen. It is a huge, deep valley separating Scotland's two mountain ranges: the Northwest Highlands and the Grampian Mountains. We traveled partway through the Glen on the Caledonian Canal, an important old trade waterway.

Loch Lochy and Glen More, the "Great Glen"

Ben Nevis and Fort William

Ben Nevis
above the loch

Ben Nevis is right nearby. That's the highest mountain in Great Britain. Its name means "mountain of snows." We took a cable-car about half-way up the mountain. What a sight! Our guide said that Glen Nevis, the beautiful valley below, has been chosen as the location for scenes in several movies.

Skye (Mallaig)

We took a short ferry ride from the bustling fishing port of Mallaig to Skye. It's the largest of the islands called the Inner Hebrides, off Scotland's northwest coast.

Even though it has unpredictable weather, Skye is one of Scotland's most popular vacation spots. It has spectacular scenery—streams, wooded glens, soaring sea cliffs, and waterfalls. It has also inspired some of the country's most beloved songs. And, when the mists lift, you can see the jagged, snow-capped peaks of the Cuillin Hills everywhere you go.

Portree Harbor, Skye

Sugaghan, Isle of Skye

Lewis

Our next stop was the Isle of Lewis and Harris. It's the largest and most northern of the 130-mile-long archipelago (island chain) called the Western Isles or Outer Hebrides. Unlike the Inner Hebrides, the barren, treeless landscapes here are a mix of windswept beaches, heather-covered hills, and marshy rolling wastelands, called moors.

Despite the harsh conditions, our guide says people have lived here for thousands of years. Today we visited the Callinish Stones. Scientists believe that these huge standing stones may have been used by early farming peoples to make astronomical predictions.

Ancient shell mound temple

Aisle of Lewis, the Callinish Stones

Orkney

Our next stop, the Orkney Islands, only became part of Scotland about 500 years ago. It was a Viking stronghold for more than 600 years. Legend has it that the islands were a wedding present from the King of Norway to the King of Scotland when he married a Norwegian princess. Independent islanders still refer to the rest of the country as "the Sooth" (south). They call themselves Orcadians rather than Scots. They even fly their own flag!

Surprisingly, the Orkney's 65 islands have a mild climate. Our guide said it's because of warm currents from the Gulf Stream. The climate and the island's rich, fertile soil make the Orkneys perfect for growing crops and raising livestock.

Orkney Islands, cliffs

Orkney Islands, port of Stromness

Orkney Islands, the ring of Brodgar

Orkney Islands, Kirkwall ruin

People have lived in this peaceful place for more than 5,000 years. More prehistoric remains have been found here than anywhere else in Scotland. Stone Age settlements have been discovered, along with great religious centers and huge group burial chambers.

Before taking the ferry back to the mainland today, we visited Stromness. This place has been an important port for centuries. Herring and whaling expeditions sailed from here, and ships from all over the world docked here before setting out for the New World.

Oban and Mull

Next we traveled to Oban, a resort located on Scotland's southwest coast. Oban means "bay." Its sheltered, crescent-shaped harbor is one of the country's most scenic. Last night we climbed to the town's famous landmark— "McCaig's Folly." It's an unfinished copy of Rome's grand Colosseum.

It was a short ferry ride from Oban to the island of Mull. Like Skye, Mull is part of the Inner Hebrides. We're staying in Tobermory, a tiny fishing port. Brightly colored houses and shops nestle along the curved harbor, which is supposed to contain a sunken treasure ship!

Oban, the port to Mull

Tobermory, Mull

Oban Castle Estate

Oban

Touring Mull, the rainiest of the Hebrides, can get wet. The beautiful countryside is wild and varied. There are sandy beaches and gently rolling pasturelands. There are also bleak moors, and a great extinct volcano—Ben More—the island's highest peak. Yesterday we visited MacKinnon's Cave, one of the deepest in the Hebrides. Legend says it's a passage to the underworld of fairies.

Glasgow

Glasgow is our last stop. It's Scotland's largest city. The city is back down south, in the Central Lowlands, where most Scots live. Glasgow is set on the banks of the River Clyde. That's the country's most important river. Ships from the Atlantic Ocean can sail right into the city.

Glasgow is the heart of Scotland's business and industry. When we left our hotel yesterday, Glaswegians (residents of Glasgow) were already crowding the city's excellent transportation system. Buses, trains, and Scotland's only subway system whisk workers to their jobs. The city is a center for television broadcasting and filmmaking. It also has factories that produce electronic equipment, chemicals, petroleum products, textiles, and heavy machinery.

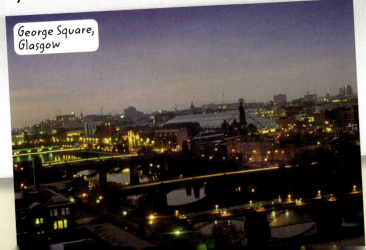

George Square, Glasgow

Bridge over the Clyde

Downtown Glasgow

Later, as we churned down the river on the world's last sea-going paddle steamer, we could see where huge shipyards once stood. For nearly a century, Glasgow was the center of the world's shipbuilding industry. Famous ships like the Queen Mary were built here. Thousands of people arrived looking for work, and terrible slums, called "gorbals," developed to house them. Today, modern housing has replaced the slums. Grimy, smoke-covered buildings have been scrubbed clean, and tourists admire Glasgow's many sights. The city's proud motto is, "Let Glasgow flourish!"

Glasgow

According to the guidebook, in 1990 Glasgow won the title of "European City of Culture"—beating out such famous cultural capitals as Paris, France and Athens, Greece!

The city is home to a historic university (the second-oldest in the country), the Scottish National Orchestra, and the Scottish Opera. It also has the Scottish Ballet and many art museums. At the famous Burrell Collection, the lifetime accumulation of a rich shipping tycoon, we saw everything from sculpture and paintings to tapestries and furniture.

McLellan Art Galleries

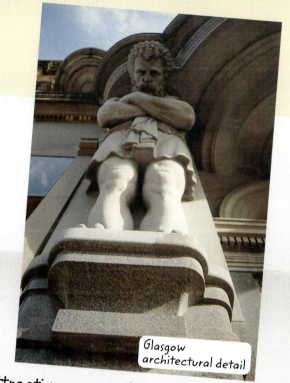

Glasgow architectural detail

The city also has attractive squares, lovely riverside promenades or walks, and more than 70 public parks.

In 1999, Glasgow beat out both Edinburgh and London to become "City of Architecture and Design." It was a tribute to its rich mix of architectural styles. On our way to a "ceilidh" (dance party), our guide pointed out a medieval cathedral; modern, glass-lined galleries; and most notably, the city's distinctive, fancy Victorian buildings.

Glossary

Ancient very old.

Distillery a place that purifies liquids by heating them until they turn into gas, and then letting them cool to form liquid again.

Glen a narrow valley.

Medieval to do with the Middle Ages, approximately A.D. 500 to 1450.

Moor an open, grassy field usually covered with heather or marshes.

Scepter a rod that was carried by kings and queens as a sign of authority.

Sonar an instrument used to detect underwater objects.

Tenement a run-down apartment building.

Thoroughfare a main road.

For More Information

Books

Department of Geography, Lerner Publications. *Scotland in Pictures*. Minneapolis, MN: Lerner Publications Group, 1991.

Hirst, Mike. *Scotland* (Origins). Danbury, CT: Franklin Watts, Inc., 1997.

Pickels, Dwayne. Arthur Schlesinger. Fred Israel. *Scottish Clans and Tartans* (Looking Into the Past). New York, NY: Chelsea House, 1997.

Web Sites

Gateway to Scotland

Learn more about the geography, history, culture, and sites of Scotland—www.geo.ed.uk/home/scotland/ scotland.html

Scotland Online

Find everything from current news to pastimes to postcards—www.scotland.net

Index